D0963138

DOVER · THRIFT · EDITIONS

Don Juan in Hell

From Man and Superman

GEORGE BERNARD SHAW

DOVER PUBLICATIONS, INC.
Mineola, New York

DOVER THRIFT EDITIONS

GENERAL EDITOR: MARY CAROLYN WALDREP
EDITOR OF THIS VOLUME: JANET BAINE KOPITO

Bibliographical Note

This Dover edition, first published in 2006, is an unabridged republication of the text of *Don Juan in Hell* (from Act III of *Man and Superman: A Comedy and a Philosophy*), as published by Brentano's, New York, in 1903. The Publisher's Note, "What—Shaw Again?" and Foreword were included in *Don Juan in Hell,* as published by Dodd, Mead & Company, New York, in 1952.

International Standard Book Number: 0-486-44845-2

Manufactured in the United States of America
Dover Publications, Inc., 31 East 2nd Street, Mineola, N.Y. 11501

WHAT—SHAW AGAIN?

Yes, because he makes it inescapable. Yes, because his deathless voice has once again brought our so-called living theatre to life. Yes, because in a season up to now cursed and largely overrun by the efforts of pygmies he has stood out like a colossus, an intellect among the thoughtless, a genius among hacks, and a seer among the blind.

It is the "Don Juan in Hell" scene from "Man and Superman," as read by Charles Laughton, Charles Boyer, Cedric Hardwicke, and Agnes Moorehead, which leaves me with no other inclination or choice than to write about Shaw. For some time now audiences in city after city up and down the United States (and England, too) have had the opportunity to enjoy this seldom performed interlude that Shaw wrote fifty years ago. Now, at last, an under-privileged New York has been permitted to respond to its excitements.

Nothing Broadway has had to offer of recent years has been more absorbing than this theatrically unorthodox presentation of a play which is not a play in the ordinary sense. The performance is in the nature of a reading. Only a shallow forestage is used and it is backed by a black curtain. In front of this curtain are microphones and stools, and music stands to hold the bound copies of the text carried in by the actors. The three men are dressed in dinner jackets and Miss Moorehead wears an evening gown. Mr. Laughton briefly and charmingly tells the essentials of the Don Juan story and announces the cast. Thereafter he leads us into the script by letting us hear Shaw's stage direction. As far as the trappings of production go, that is all. But what an all and what an evening it proves to be!

If any members of Local 829 managed to squeeze into the theatre where it is playing, they—and they alone—in a huge and rapt audience must have felt a certain discomfort. They must even have had a clearer understanding of Othello's feelings when he complained his occupation was

gone. For Local 829 is the United Scenic Artists. And here
was Shaw proving, as Shakespeare demonstrated long ago,
how unnecessary scenery is when great language sets the
stage.

Anyone can cite examples of the way in which Shakespeare relied on his pen to do the brushwork most contemporary playwrights assume will be done for them by scene
designers with the aid of dependable electricians. In "Mac-
beth" the First Murderer's "The west yet glimmers with
some streaks of day"; Horatio's "But look, the morn, in
russet mantle clad, Walks o'er the dew of yon high east-
ward hill . . ."; Lorenzo's "The moon shines bright. In
such a night as this, When the sweet wind did gently kiss
the trees And they did make no noise . . ."; and Lear's
"Blow, winds, and crack your cheeks! rage! blow! You
cataracts and hurricanoes, spout . . ." are familiar instances of the kind of verbal scenery Shakespeare supplied
in play after play.

Shaw's employment of the language proves no less self-
sufficient in this uncostumed and unset "reading" of "Don
Juan in Hell." Yet there is a striking difference. Shaw has
no interest in conjuring images to evoke a physical setting.
He makes fun of Dante for having described hell as a place
of mud, frost, filth, fire, and venomous serpents. He is
equally contemptuous of Milton for having introduced can-
non and gunpowder as a means of expelling the Devil from
heaven. Shaw's hell is visually nonexistent. In his own
words "there is nothing; omnipresent nothing. No sky, no
peaks, no light, no sound, no time nor space, utter void."
There is only somewhere the faint throbbing buzz of a
Mozartian strain and a pallor which "reveals a man in
the void, an incorporeal but visible man, seated, absurdly
enough, on nothing."

In the course of "Don Juan" Shaw pays tribute to the
wonders of that slowly evolved bodily organ, the eye,
which has permitted the living organism to "see where it
was going and what was coming to help or threaten it." But

his concern is with neither the eye nor the visible world. Instead, it is with the evolving mind's eye and its higher plane of vision which should enable us to see "the purpose of Life." He makes his hell a void so that he can fill it with ideas. His intellect sets the stage; his fervor and his wit light it. What absorbs his attention and ours is not a place but the plight of Man. It is Man's foolishness and his potentialities; what he has been, what he is, and what he must become if he is either to justify his existence or safeguard his survival.

There are those beyond counting who expect a play to have a plot. They want it at least to tell how Jack gets Jill or Jill Jack. The story of Ann Whitefield's pursuit and conquest of John Tanner is the narrative basis of "Man and Superman," into the third act of which "Don Juan in Hell" is tucked as a detachable dream sequence. Being spirits, the characters in this interlude are no longer plot-bound. Having already lived their personal histories, the Devil, the Commander, Doña Ana, and Don Juan are free in hell to concentrate on a far larger, more universal story—the story of Mankind. This is the subject of their dialogue. To be more accurate, it is the theme of their "great debate." Although they do nothing except talk, such talk is in itself an exciting activity. The very thrust and fascination of their arguments create drama. Due to the mind at work, this battle of ideas is far more dramatic in its action than a thousand trumped-up plots.

Shaw's hell has nothing in common with the hell that fires the imagination of those who hit the sawdust trail. It is not even the satanic realm with which milder ministers are fond of threatening sinners. Instead, it is as unconventional an inferno as only Shaw could make it. He establishes it as a delightful retreat for seekers after happiness who intellectually and spiritually have not outgrown its pleasures. Its pleasures are such that it is visited frequently by those who are bored with heaven. Needless to say, Shaw's heaven is no less exceptional than his hell. His heaven is open only to those who have become the masters of reality. This sets it very much apart from earth, where mortals are reality's slaves. In this Shavian paradise what is done cannot be undone by repentance and spoken words cannot be unspoken by withdrawing them, any more than the truth can be annihilated by a general agreement to give it the lie.

One of Shaw's most typical and engaging paradoxes is that such a heaven attracts, of all people, Don Juan the libertine. Juan has tired of the license which won him earthly fame and comes to see the emptiness of the diversions offered him in hell. His belief in Man is greater than the Devil's disbelief. The Devil may argue against heaven and Man with all the skill at Shaw's command, but it is to this heavenly refuge of realists that Don Juan is determined to go. And go he finally does, as the champion of the Life Force, Creative Evolution, and the Superman.

Most readers and playgoers remember lines from Shaw's memorable preface to "Man and Superman," from the play and the interlude, or from "The Revolutionist's Handbook," which concludes the volume. None of Shaw's works bulges with more passages which refuse to be forgotten and cry to be quoted. His mind never had freer play than in "Don Juan in Hell." His prowess as a debater was never more irrefutably established than in the discussion where the voices of Shaw and Anti-Shaw are heard, and each is given the benefit of all Shaw's eloquence, wit, and moral passion. Following such an argument may make hard demands on those unable to concentrate and antagonistic to thought. But in spite of GBS's confessed wordiness, listening, to anyone with half a mind, has seldom been easier or more rewarding.

One of the incredible aspects of "Don Juan in Hell" is that it remains utterly and urgently contemporary. The half-century which has passed since it was written has left it undated. Take, for example, the Devil's speech in the first part of the evening when he appears to have the better of the debate. Don Juan has claimed that Man's hope lies in his brain. "And is Man any the less destroying himself for all this boasted brain of his?" asks the Devil. "Have you walked up and down upon the earth lately? I have; and I have examined Man's wonderful inventions. And I tell you that in the arts of life man invents nothing; but in the arts of death he outdoes Nature herself, and produces by chemistry and machinery all the slaughter of plague, pestilence, and famine. The peasant I tempt today eats and drinks what was eaten and drunk by the peasants of ten thousand years ago; and the house he lives in has not altered as much in a thousand centuries as the fashion of a lady's bonnet in a score of weeks. But when he goes out to slay, he carries a marvel of mechanism that lets loose at the touch of his finger all the hidden molecular energies, and leaves the javelin, the arrow, the blowpipe of his fathers far behind. In the arts of peace Man is a bungler."

Towards the end of the present "reading," divided as it is into two parts so as to ease the strain of taut listening, Don Juan speaks not only for himself but for Shaw. "I tell you," he insists, "that as long as I can conceive something better than myself I cannot be easy unless I am striving to bring it into existence or clearing the way for it. That is the law of my life. That is the working within me of Life's incessant aspiration to higher organization, wider, deeper, intenser self-consciousness, and clearer self-understanding. It was the supremacy of this purpose that reduced love for me to the mere pleasure of a moment, art for me to the mere schooling of my faculties, religion for me to a mere excuse for laziness, since it had set up a God who looked at the world and saw that it was good, against the instinct in me that looked through my eyes at the world and saw that it could be improved. I tell you that in the pursuit of my own pleasure, my own health, my own fortune, I have never known happiness."

Thus the Don Juan-Shaw—entirely uncynical. Thus, Shaw, the philosophic man, with all his energies in revolt against the wrong or the merely adequate, and mobilized in a campaign for improvement. Thus Shaw, the militant reformer, the wrecker who destroys to rebuild, the firm believer in the "continual ascent of Man on the stepping stones of his dead selves to higher things." Thus Shaw with his conviction that Man's need and hope lie in evolving into a being better than he now is. Thus Shaw with his extension of the theory of the Superman which he derived from Nietzsche, who, though named in the original text, is for some strange reason left unmentioned in the present version.

The performance "Don Juan" is given is far more than a reading and in every respect worthy of Shaw's writing. Although it has an irresistible informality, it can claim a splendid dignity. Among its igniting qualities count the fact that it puts the imagination to stimulating work at the same time that it keeps the mind racing with delight. The members of the Quartette read from memory rather than from their texts. This is what makes "reading" so inadequate a word as a description of the presentation.

Surely, no dramatic critic has performed for the theatre a finer service than A. B. Walkley's when he urged Shaw to write a drama about Don Juan. No less surely, few contemporary actors have performed a greater service to Shaw, the theatre, and all of us than this Quartette of excellent actors by letting us see and hear "Don Juan in Hell."

—JOHN MASON BROWN.

FOREWORD

I first read this piece when I was a student of dramatic art in London in 1927. I had been singled out by Shaw at a rehearsal and had loyally set out to read all his works. The second one I came up against was Man and Superman, and this scene. After the first shocks I went around dreaming what a wonderful world it would be in which audiences would come to see this. Well, here we are, and it isn't!

I did not understand any of the references to the Don Juan legend. I was expensively educated, but nobody had shown me how to go to a public library and look things up in books, so I escaped into thinking that such grand things were not for ordinary people like me. In order that you will have no chance to creep into that hard shell, here is all of the legend necessary to be able to follow this piece.

Don Juan is the man who loves too many women and leaves them. The basic story on which the early Spanish play and the Molière play and the Mozart opera are founded goes something like this: Don Juan once made love to a woman called Donna Ana. Donna Ana was married to a man called Ottavio. You will read about him in this piece. He does not appear.

So when Don Juan made love to Donna Ana, Donna Ana screamed, and her father came to her rescue to defend her virtue. Donna Ana's father got into a sword fight with Don Juan, and in the sword fight Don Juan killed Donna Ana's father. Then the story cuts to some time later. There was a statue erected to the memory of Donna Ana's father, and in a high mood one day Don Juan invited the Statue to come and have supper with him, and lo and behold, the Statue stepped down from its pedestal and came and had supper with Don Juan. And in return the Statue invited Don Juan to supper with it, and on this occasion the Statue took Don Juan down into Hell, where, according to Shaw, Ana joins them and they talk with the Devil.

—CHARLES LAUGHTON

PUBLISHER'S NOTE

The Don Juan in Hell episode occurs near the close of the third act of Man and Superman and is here reproduced in the original text.

Straker snores; rolls over on his side; and relapses into sleep. Stillness settles on the Sierra; and the darkness deepens. The fire has again buried itself in white ash and ceased to glow. The peaks shew unfathomably dark against the starry firmament; but now the stars dim and vanish; and the sky seems to steal away out of the universe. Instead of the Sierra there is nothing: omnipresent nothing. No sky, no peaks, no light, no sound, no time nor space, utter void. Then somewhere the beginning of a pallor, and with it a faint throbbing buzz as of a ghostly violoncello palpitating on the same note endlessly. A couple of ghostly violins presently take advantage of this bass

and therewith the pallor reveals a man in the void, an incorporeal but visible man, seated, absurdly enough, on nothing. For a moment he raises his head as the music passes him by. Then, with a heavy sigh, he droops in utter dejection; and the violins, discouraged, retrace their melody in despair and at last give it up, extinguished by wailings from uncanny wind instruments, thus:—

1

It is all very odd. One recognizes the Mozartian strain; and on this hint, and by the aid of certain sparkles of violet light in the pallor, the man's costume explains itself as that of a Spanish nobleman of the XV-XVI century. Don Juan, of course; but where? why? how? Besides, in the brief lifting of his face, now hidden by his hat brim, there was a curious suggestion of Tanner. A more critical, fastidious, handsome face, paler and colder, without Tanner's impetuous credulity and enthusiasm, and without a touch of his modern plutocratic vulgarity, but still a resemblance, even an identity. The name too: Don Juan Tenorio, John Tanner. Where on earth—or elsewhere—have we got to from the XX century and the Sierra?

Another pallor in the void, this time not violet, but a disagreeable smoky yellow. With it, the whisper of a ghostly clarionet turning this tune into infinite sadness:

The yellowish pallor moves: there is an old crone wandering in the void, bent and toothless; draped, as well as one can guess, in the coarse brown frock of some religious order. She wanders and wanders in her slow hopeless way, much as a wasp flies in its rapid busy way, until she blunders against the thing she seeks: companionship. With a sob of relief the poor old creature clutches at the presence of the man and addresses him in her dry unlovely voice, which can still express pride and resolution as well as suffering.

THE OLD WOMAN. Excuse me; but I am so lonely; and this place is so awful.

DON JUAN. A new comer?

THE OLD WOMAN. Yes: I suppose I died this morning. I confessed; I had extreme unction; I was in bed with my family about me and my eyes fixed on the cross. Then it grew dark; and when the light came back it was this light by which I walk seeing nothing. I have wandered for hours in horrible loneliness.

DON JUAN [*sighing*] Ah! you have not yet lost the sense of time. One soon does, in eternity.

THE OLD WOMAN. Where are we?

DON JUAN. In hell.

THE OLD WOMAN [*proudly*] Hell! I in hell! How dare you?

DON JUAN [*unimpressed*] Why not, Señora?

THE OLD WOMAN. You do not know to whom you are speaking. I am a lady, and a faithful daughter of the Church.

DON JUAN. I do not doubt it.

THE OLD WOMAN. But how then can I be in hell? Purgatory, perhaps: I have not been perfect: who has? But hell! oh, you are lying.

DON JUAN. Hell, Señora, I assure you; hell at its best: that is, its most solitary—though perhaps you would prefer company.

THE OLD WOMAN. But I have sincerely repented; I have confessed—

DON JUAN. How much?

THE OLD WOMAN. More sins than I really committed. I loved confession.

DON JUAN. Ah, that is perhaps as bad as confessing too little. At all events, Señora, whether by oversight or intention, you are certainly damned, like myself; and there is nothing for it now but to make the best of it.

THE OLD WOMAN [*indignantly*] Oh! and I might have been so much wickeder! All my good deeds wasted! It is unjust.

DON JUAN. No: you were fully and clearly warned. For your bad deeds, vicarious atonement, mercy without justice. For your good deeds, justice without mercy. We have many good people here.

THE OLD WOMAN. Were you a good man?

DON JUAN. I was a murderer.

THE OLD WOMAN. A murderer! Oh, how dare they send me to herd with murderers! I was not as bad as that: I was a good woman. There is some mistake: where can I have it set right?

DON JUAN. I do not know whether mistakes can be corrected here. Probably they will not admit a mistake even if they have made one.

THE OLD WOMAN. But whom can I ask?

DON JUAN. I should ask the Devil, Señora: he understands the ways of this place, which is more than I ever could.

THE OLD WOMAN. The Devil! *I* speak to the Devil!

DON JUAN. In hell, Señora, the Devil is the leader of the best society.

THE OLD WOMAN. I tell you, wretch, I know I am not in hell.

DON JUAN. How do you know?

THE OLD WOMAN. Because I feel no pain.

DON JUAN. Oh, then there is no mistake: you are intentionally damned.

THE OLD WOMAN. Why do you say that?

DON JUAN. Because hell, Señora, is a place for the wicked. The wicked are quite comfortable in it: it was made for them. You tell me you feel no pain. I conclude you are one of those for whom Hell exists.

THE OLD WOMAN. Do you feel no pain?

DON JUAN. I am not one of the wicked, Señora; therefore it bores me, bores me beyond description, beyond belief.

THE OLD WOMAN. Not one of the wicked! You said you were a murderer.

DON JUAN. Only a duel. I ran my sword through an old man who was trying to run his through me.

THE OLD WOMAN. If you were a gentleman, that was not a murder.

DON JUAN. The old man called it murder, because he was, he said, defending his daughter's honor. By this he meant that because I foolishly fell in love with her and told her so, she screamed; and he tried to assassinate me after calling me insulting names.

THE OLD WOMAN. You were like all men. Libertines and

murderers all, all, all!

DON JUAN. And yet we meet here, dear lady.

THE OLD WOMAN. Listen to me. My father was slain by just such a wretch as you, in just such a duel, for just such a cause. I screamed: it was my duty. My father drew on my assailant: his honor demanded it. He fell: that was the reward of honor. I am here: in hell, you tell me: that is the reward of duty. Is there justice in heaven?

DON JUAN. No; but there is justice in hell: heaven is far above such idle human personalities. You will be welcome in hell, Señora. Hell is the home of honor, duty, justice, and the rest of the seven deadly virtues. All the wickedness on earth is done in their name: where else but in hell should they have their reward? Have I not told you that the truly damned are those who are happy in hell?

THE OLD WOMAN. And are you happy here?

DON JUAN [*springing to his feet*] No; and that is the enigma on which I ponder in darkness. Why am I here? I, who repudiated all duty, trampled honor underfoot, and laughed at justice!

THE OLD WOMAN. Oh, what do I care why you are here? Why am *I* here? I, who sacrificed all my inclinations to womanly virtue and propriety!

DON JUAN. Patience, lady: you will be perfectly happy and at home here. As saith the poet, "Hell is a city much like Seville."

THE OLD WOMAN. Happy! here! where I am nothing! where I am nobody!

DON JUAN. Not at all: you are a lady; and wherever ladies are is hell. Do not be surprised or terrified: you will find everything here that a lady can desire, including devils who will serve you from sheer love of servitude, and magnify your importance for the sake of dignifying their service— the best of servants.

THE OLD WOMAN. My servants will be devils!

DON JUAN. Have you ever had servants who were not devils?

THE OLD WOMAN. Never: they were devils, perfect devils, all of them. But that is only a manner of speaking. I thought you meant that my servants here would be real devils.

DON JUAN. No more real devils than you will be a real lady. Nothing is real here. That is the horror of damnation.

THE OLD WOMAN. Oh, this is all madness. This is worse than fire and the worm.

DON JUAN. For you, perhaps, there are consolations. For instance: how old were you when you changed from time to eternity?

THE OLD WOMAN. Do not ask me how old I was—as if I were a thing of the past. I am 77.

DON JUAN. A ripe age, Señora. But in hell old age is not tolerated. It is too real. Here we worship Love and Beauty. Our souls being entirely damned, we cultivate our hearts. As a lady of 77, you would not have a single acquaintance in hell.

THE OLD WOMAN. How can I help my age, man?

DON JUAN. You forget that you have left your age behind you in the realm of time. You are no more 77 than you are 7 or 17 or 27.

THE OLD WOMAN. Nonsense!

DON JUAN. Consider, Señora: was not this true even when you lived on earth? When you were 70, were you really older underneath your wrinkles and your grey hairs than when you were 30?

THE OLD WOMAN. No, younger: at 30 I was a fool. But of what use is it to feel younger and look older?

DON JUAN. You see, Señora, the look was only an illusion. Your wrinkles lied, just as the plump smooth skin of many a stupid girl of 17, with heavy spirits and decrepit ideas, lies about her age? Well, here we have no bodies: we see each other as bodies only because we learnt to think about one another under that aspect when we were alive; and we still think in that way, knowing no other. But we can appear to one another at what age we choose. You have but to will any of your old looks back, and back they will come.

THE OLD WOMAN. It cannot be true.

DON JUAN. Try.

THE OLD WOMAN. Seventeen!

DON JUAN. Stop. Before you decide, I had better tell you that these things are a matter of fashion. Occasionally we have a rage for 17; but it does not last long. Just at present the fashionable age is 40—or say 37; but there are signs of a change. If you were at all good-looking at 27, I should suggest your trying that, and setting a new fashion.

THE OLD WOMAN. I do not believe a word you are saying. However, 27 be it. [*Whisk! the old woman becomes a young one, magnificently attired, and so handsome that in the radiance into which her dull yellow halo has suddenly lightened one might almost mistake her for Ann Whitefield*].

DON JUAN. Doña Ana de Ulloa!

ANA. What? You know me!

DON JUAN. And you forget me!

ANA. I cannot see your face. [*He raises his hat*]. Don Juan Tenorio! Monster! You who slew my father! even here you pursue me.

DON JUAN. I protest I do not pursue you. Allow me to withdraw [*going*].

ANA [*seizing his arm*] You shall not leave me alone in this dreadful place.

DON JUAN. Provided my staying be not interpreted as pursuit.

ANA [*releasing him*] You may well wonder how I can endure your presence. My dear, dear father!

DON JUAN. Would you like to see him?

ANA. My father here!!!

DON JUAN. No: he is in heaven.

ANA. I knew it. My noble father! He is looking down on us now. What must he feel to see his daughter in this place, and in conversation with his murderer!

DON JUAN. By the way, if we should meet him—

ANA. How can we meet him? He is in heaven.

DON JUAN. He condescends to look in upon us here from

time to time. Heaven bores him. So let me warn you that if you meet him he will be mortally offended if you speak of me as his murderer! He maintains that he was a much better swordsman than I, and that if his foot had not slipped he would have killed me. No doubt he is right: I was not a good fencer. I never dispute the point; so we are excellent friends.

ANA. It is no dishonor to a soldier to be proud of his skill in arms.

DON JUAN. You would rather not meet him, probably.

ANA. How dare you say that?

DON JUAN. Oh, that is the usual feeling here. You may remember that on earth—though of course we never confessed it—the death of anyone we knew, even those we liked best, was always mingled with a certain satisfaction at being finally done with them.

ANA. Monster! Never, never.

DON JUAN [*placidly*] I see you recognize the feeling. Yes: a funeral was always a festivity in black, especially the funeral of a relative. At all events, family ties are rarely kept up here. Your father is quite accustomed to this: he will not expect any devotion from you.

ANA. Wretch: I wore mourning for him all my life.

DON JUAN. Yes: it became you. But a life of mourning is one thing: an eternity of it quite another. Besides, here you are as dead as he. Can anything be more ridiculous than one dead person mourning for another? Do not look shocked, my dear Ana; and do not be alarmed: there is plenty of humbug in hell (indeed there is hardly anything else); but the humbug of death and age and change is dropped because here we are all dead and all eternal. You will pick up our ways soon.

ANA. And will all the men call me their dear Ana?

DON JUAN. No. That was a slip of the tongue. I beg your pardon.

ANA [*almost tenderly*] Juan: did you really love me when you behaved so disgracefully to me?

DON JUAN [*impatiently*] Oh, I beg you not to begin talking about love. Here they talk of nothing else but love: its beauty, its holiness, its spirituality, its devil knows what!—excuse me; but it does so bore me. They dont know what theyre talking about: I do. They think they have achieved the perfection of love because they have no bodies. Sheer imaginative debauchery! Faugh!

ANA. Has even death failed to refine your soul, Juan? Has the terrible judgment of which my father's statue was the minister taught you no reverence?

DON JUAN. How is that very flattering statue, by the way? Does it still come to supper with naughty people and cast them into this bottomless pit?

ANA. It has been a great expense to me. The boys in the monastery school would not let it alone: the mischievous ones broke it; and the studious ones wrote their names on it. Three new noses in two years, and fingers without end. I had to leave it to its fate at last; and now I fear it is shockingly mutilated. My poor father!

DON JUAN. Hush! Listen! [*Two great chords rolling on syncopated waves of sound break forth: D minor and its dominant: a sound of dreadful joy to all musicians*]. Ha! Mozart's statue music. It is your father. You had better disappear until I prepare him. [*She vanishes*].

From the void comes a living statue of white marble, designed to represent a majestic old man. But he waives his majesty with infinite grace; walks with a feather-like step; and makes every wrinkle in his war worn visage brim over with holiday joyousness. To his sculptor he owes a perfectly trained figure, which he carries erect and trim; and the ends of his moustache curl up, elastic as watchsprings, giving him an air which, but for its Spanish dignity, would be called jaunty. He is on the pleasantest terms with Don Juan. His voice, save for a much more distinguished intonation, is so like the voice of Roebuck Ramsden that it calls attention to the fact that they are not unlike one another in spite of their very different fashions of shaving.

DON JUAN. Ah, here you are, my friend. Why dont you learn to sing the splendid music Mozart has written for you?

THE STATUE. Unluckily he has written it for a bass voice. Mine is a counter tenor. Well: have you repented yet?

DON JUAN. I have too much consideration for you to repent, Don Gonzalo. If I did, you would have no excuse for coming from Heaven to argue with me.

THE STATUE. True. Remain obdurate, my boy. I wish I had killed you, as I should have done but for an accident. Then I should have come here; and you would have had a statue and a reputation for piety to live up to. Any news?

DON JUAN. Yes: your daughter is dead.

THE STATUE [*puzzled*] My daughter? [*Recollecting*] Oh! the one you were taken with. Let me see: what was her name?

DON JUAN. Ana.

THE STATUE. To be sure: Ana. A goodlooking girl, if I recollect aright. Have you warned Whatshisname? her husband.

DON JUAN. My friend Ottavio? No: I have not seen him since Ana arrived.

Ana comes indignantly to light.

ANA. What does this mean? Ottavio here and your friend! And you, father, have forgotten my name. You are indeed turned to stone.

THE STATUE. My dear: I am so much more admired in marble than I ever was in my own person that I have retained the shape the sculptor gave me. He was one of the first men of his day: you must acknowledge that.

ANA. Father! Vanity! personal vanity! from you!

THE STATUE. Ah, you outlived that weakness, my daughter: you must be nearly 80 by this time. I was cut off (by an accident) in my 64th year, and am considerably your junior in consequence. Besides, my child, in this place, what our libertine friend here would call the farce of parental wisdom is dropped. Regard me, I beg, as a fellow creature, not as a father.

ANA. You speak as this villain speaks.

THE STATUE. Juan is a sound thinker, Ana. A bad fencer,

but a sound thinker.

ANA [*horror creeping upon her*] I begin to understand. These are devils, mocking me. I had better pray.

THE STATUE [*consoling her*] No, no, no, my child: do not pray. If you do, you will throw away the main advantage of this place. Written over the gate here are the words "Leave every hope behind, ye who enter." Only think what a relief that is! For what is hope? A form of moral responsibility. Here there is no hope, and consequently no duty, no work, nothing to be gained by praying, nothing to be lost by doing what you like. Hell, in short, is a place where you have nothing to do but amuse yourself. [*Don Juan sighs deeply*]. You sigh, friend Juan; but if you dwelt in heaven, as I do, you would realize your advantages.

DON JUAN. You are in good spirits today, Commander. You are positively brilliant. What is the matter?

THE STATUE. I have come to a momentous decision, my boy. But first, where is our friend the Devil? I must consult him in the matter. And Ana would like to make his acquaintance, no doubt.

ANA. You are preparing some torment for me.

DON JUAN. All that is superstition, Ana. Reassure yourself. Remember: the devil is not so black as he is painted.

THE STATUE. Let us give him a call.

At the wave of the statue's hand the great chords roll out again; but this time Mozart's music gets grotesquely adulterated with Gounod's. A scarlet halo begins to glow; and into it the Devil rises, very Mephistophelean, and not at all unlike Mendoza, though not so interesting. He looks older; is getting prematurely bald; and, in spite of an effusion of goodnature and friendliness, is peevish and sensitive when his advances are not reciprocated. He does not inspire much confidence in his powers of hard work or endurance, and is, on the whole, a disagreeably self-indulgent looking person; but he is clever and plausible, though perceptibly less well bred than the two other men, and enormously less vital than the woman.

THE DEVIL [*heartily*] Have I the pleasure of again receiving a visit from the illustrious Commander of Calatrava? [*Coldly*] Don Juan, your servant. [*Politely*] And a strange lady? My respects, Señora.

ANA. Are you—

THE DEVIL [*bowing*] Lucifer, at your service.

ANA. I shall go mad.

THE DEVIL [*gallantly*] Ah, Señora, do not be anxious. You come to us from earth, full of the prejudices and terrors of that priest-ridden place. You have heard me ill spoken of; and yet, believe me, I have hosts of friends there.

ANA. Yes: you reign in their hearts.

THE DEVIL [*shaking his head*] You flatter me, Señora; but you are mistaken. It is true that the world cannot get on without me; but it never gives me credit for that: in its heart it mistrusts and hates me. Its sympathies are all with misery, with poverty, with starvation of the body and of the heart. I call on it to sympathize with joy, with love, with happiness, with beauty—

DON JUAN [*nauseated*] Excuse me: I am going. You know I cannot stand this.

THE DEVIL [*angrily*] Yes: I know that you are no friend of mine.

THE STATUE. What harm is he doing you, Juan? It seems to me that he was talking excellent sense when you interrupted him.

THE DEVIL [*warmly patting the statue's hand*] Thank you, my friend: thank you. You have always understood me: he has always disparaged and avoided me.

DON JUAN. I have treated you with perfect courtesy.

THE DEVIL. Courtesy! What is courtesy? I care nothing for mere courtesy. Give me warmth of heart, true sincerity, the bond of sympathy with love and joy—

DON JUAN. You are making me ill.

THE DEVIL. There! [*Appealing to the statue*] You hear, sir! Oh, by what irony of fate was this cold selfish egotist sent to my kingdom, and you taken to the icy mansions of the sky!

THE STATUE. I cant complain. I was a hypocrite; and it

served me right to be sent to heaven.

THE DEVIL. Why, sir, do you not join us, and leave a sphere for which your temperament is too sympathetic, your heart too warm, your capacity for enjoyment too generous?

THE STATUE. I have this day resolved to do so. In future, excellent Son of the Morning, I am yours. I have left Heaven for ever.

THE DEVIL [*again touching the marble hand*] Ah, what an honor! what a triumph for our cause! Thank you, thank you. And now, my friend—I may call you so at last—could you not persuade him to take the place you have left vacant above?

THE STATUE [*shaking his head*] I cannot conscientiously recommend anybody with whom I am on friendly terms to deliberately make himself dull and uncomfortable.

THE DEVIL. Of course not; but are you sure he would be uncomfortable? Of course you know best: you brought him here originally; and we had the greatest hopes of him. His sentiments were in the best taste of our best people. You remember how he sang? [*He begins to sing in a nasal operatic baritone, tremulous from an eternity of misuse in the French manner*]

> Vivan le femmine!
> Viva il buon vino!

THE STATUE [*taking up the tune an octave higher in his counter tenor*]

> Sostegno e gloria
> D'umanità.

THE DEVIL. Precisely. Well, he never sings for us now.

DON JUAN. Do you complain of that? Hell is full of musical amateurs: music is the brandy of the damned. May not one lost soul be permitted to abstain?

THE DEVIL. You dare blaspheme against the sublimest of the arts!

DON JUAN [*with cold disgust*] You talk like a hysterical woman fawning on a fiddler.

THE DEVIL. I am not angry. I merely pity you. You have

no soul; and you are unconscious of all that you lose. Now you, Señor Commander, are a born musician. How well you sing! Mozart would be delighted if he were still here; but he moped and went to heaven. Curious how these clever men, whom you would have supposed born to be popular here, have turned out social failures, like Don Juan!

DON JUAN. I am really very sorry to be a social failure.

THE DEVIL. Not that we dont admire your intellect, you know. We do. But I look at the matter from your own point of view. You dont get on with us. The place doesnt suit you. The truth is, you have—I wont say no heart; for we know that beneath all your affected cynicism you have a warm one—

DON JUAN [*shrinking*] Dont, please dont.

THE DEVIL [*nettled*] Well, youve no capacity for enjoyment. Will that satisfy you?

DON JUAN. It is a somewhat less insufferable form of cant than the other. But if youll allow me, I'll take refuge, as usual, in solitude.

THE DEVIL. Why not take refuge in Heaven? Thats the proper place for you. [*To Ana*] Come, Señora! could you not persuade him for his own good to try change of air?

ANA. But can he go to Heaven if he wants to?

THE DEVIL. Whats to prevent him?

ANA. Can anybody—can *I* go to Heaven if I want to?

THE DEVIL [*rather contemptuously*] Certainly, if your taste lies that way.

ANA. But why doesnt everybody go to Heaven, then?

THE STATUE [*chuckling*] *I* can tell you that, my dear. It's because heaven is the most angelically dull place in all creation: thats why.

THE DEVIL. His excellency the Commander puts it with military bluntness; but the strain of living in Heaven is intolerable. There is a notion that I was turned out of it; but as a matter of fact nothing could have induced me to stay there. I simply left it and organized this place.

THE STATUE. I dont wonder at it. Nobody could stand an

eternity of heaven.

THE DEVIL. Oh, it suits some people. Let us be just, Commander: it is a question of temperament. I dont admire the heavenly temperament: I dont understand it: I dont know that I particularly want to understand it; but it takes all sorts to make a universe. There is no accounting for tastes: there are people who like it. I think Don Juan would like it.

DON JUAN. But—pardon my frankness—could you really go back there if you desired to; or are the grapes sour?

THE DEVIL. Back there! I often go back there. Have you never read the book of Job? Have you any canonical authority for assuming that there is any barrier between our circle and the other one?

ANA. But surely there is a great gulf fixed.

THE DEVIL. Dear lady: a parable must not be taken literally. The gulf is the difference between the angelic and the diabolic temperament. What more impassable gulf could you have? Think of what you have seen on earth. There is no physical gulf between the philosopher's class room and the bull ring; but the bull fighters do not come to the class room for all that. Have you ever been in the country where I have the largest following? England. There they have great racecourses, and also concert rooms where they play the classical compositions of his Excellency's friend Mozart. Those who go to the racecourses can stay away from them and go to the classical concerts instead if they like: there is no law against it; for Englishmen never will be slaves: they are free to do whatever the Government and public opinion allow them to do. And the classical concert is admitted to be a higher, more cultivated, poetic, intellectual, ennobling place than the racecourse. But do the lovers of racing desert their sport and flock to the concert room? Not they. They would suffer there all the weariness the Commander has suffered in heaven. There is the great gulf of the parable between the two places. A mere physical gulf they could bridge; or at least I could bridge it for them (the earth is full of Devil's Bridges); but the gulf of dislike is impassable and eternal. And that is the only gulf that separates my friends here from those who are invidiously called the blest.

ANA. I shall go to heaven at once.

THE STATUE. My child: one word of warning first. Let me complete my friend Lucifer's similitude of the classical concert. At every one of those concerts in England you will find rows of weary people who are there, not because they really like classical music, but because they think they ought to like it. Well, there is the same thing in heaven. A number of people sit there in glory, not because they are happy, but because they think they owe it to their position to be in heaven. They are almost all English.

THE DEVIL. Yes: the Southerners give it up and join me just as you have done. But the English really do not seem to know when they are thoroughly miserable. An Englishman thinks he is moral when he is only uncomfortable.

THE STATUE. In short, my daughter, if you go to Heaven without being naturally qualified for it, you will not enjoy yourself there.

ANA. And who dares say that I am not naturally qualified for it? The most distinguished princes of the Church have never questioned it. I owe it to myself to leave this place at once.

THE DEVIL [*offended*] As you please, Señora. I should have expected better taste from you.

ANA. Father: I shall expect you to come with me. You cannot stay here. What will people say?

THE STATUE. People! Why, the best people are here— princes of the church and all. So few go to Heaven, and so many come here, that the blest, once called a heavenly host, are a continually dwindling minority. The saints, the fathers, the elect of long ago are the cranks, the faddists, the outsiders of today.

THE DEVIL. It is true. From the beginning of my career I knew that I should win in the long run by sheer weight of public opinion, in spite of the long campaign of misrepresentation and calumny against me. At bottom the universe is a constitutional one; and with such a majority as mine I cannot be kept permanently out of office.

DON JUAN. I think, Ana, you had better stay here.

ANA [*jealously*] You do not want me to go with you.

DON JUAN. Surely you do not want to enter Heaven in the company of a reprobate like me.

ANA. All souls are equally precious. You repent, do you not?

DON JUAN. My dear Ana, you are silly. Do you suppose heaven is like earth, where people persuade themselves that what is done can be undone by repentance; that what is spoken can be unspoken by withdrawing it; that what is true can be annihilated by a general agreement to give it the lie? No: heaven is the home of the masters of reality: that is why I am going thither.

ANA. Thank you: I am going to heaven for happiness. I have had quite enough of reality on earth.

DON JUAN. Then you must stay here; for hell is the home of the unreal and of the seekers for happiness. It is the only refuge from heaven, which is, as I tell you, the home of the masters of reality, and from earth, which is the home of the slaves of reality. The earth is a nursery in which men and women play at being heroes and heroines, saints and sinners; but they are dragged down from their fool's paradise by their bodies: hunger and cold and thirst, age and decay and disease, death above all, make them slaves of reality: thrice a day meals must be eaten and digested: thrice a century a new generation must be engendered: ages of faith, of romance, and of science are all driven at last to have but one prayer "Make me a healthy animal." But here you escape this tyranny of the flesh; for here you are not an animal at all: you are a ghost, an appearance, an illusion, a convention, deathless, ageless: in a word, bodiless. There are no social questions here, no political questions, no religious questions, best of all, perhaps, no sanitary questions. Here you call your appearance beauty, your emotions love, your senti-ments heroism, your aspirations virtue, just as you did on earth; but here there are no hard facts to contradict you, no ironic contrast of your needs with your pretensions, no human comedy, nothing but a perpetual romance, a universal melodrama. As our German friend put it in his poem, "the poetically nonsensical here is good sense; and the Eternal Feminine draws us ever upward and on"—without getting us a step farther. And yet you want to leave this paradise!

ANA. But if Hell be so beautiful as this, how glorious must heaven be!

The Devil, the Statue, and Don Juan all begin to speak at once in violent protest; then stop abashed.

DON JUAN. I beg your pardon.

THE DEVIL. Not at all. I interrupted you.

THE STATUE. You were going to say something.

DON JUAN. After you, gentlemen.

THE DEVIL [*to Don Juan*] You have been so eloquent on the advantages of my dominions that I leave you to do equal justice to the drawbacks of the alternative establishment.

DON JUAN. In Heaven, as I picture it, dear lady, you live and work instead of playing and pretending. You face things as they are; you escape nothing but glamor; and your steadfastness and your peril are your glory. If the play still goes on here and on earth, and all the world is a stage, Heaven is at least behind the scenes. But Heaven cannot be described by metaphor. Thither I shall go presently, because there I hope to escape at last from lies and from the tedious, vulgar pursuit of happiness, to spend my eons in contemplation—

THE STATUE. Ugh!

DON JUAN. Señor Commander: I do not blame your disgust: a picture gallery is a dull place for a blind man. But even as you enjoy the contemplation of such romantic mirages as beauty and pleasure; so would I enjoy the contemplation of that which interests me above all things: namely, Life: the force that ever strives to attain greater power of contemplating itself. What made this brain of mine, do you think? Not the need to move my limbs; for a rat with half my brains moves as well as I. Not merely the need to do, but the need to know what I do, lest in my blind efforts to live I should be slaying myself.

THE STATUE. You would have slain yourself in your blind efforts to fence but for my foot slipping, my friend.

DON JUAN. Audacious ribald: your laughter will finish in hideous boredom before morning.

THE STATUE. Ha ha! Do you remember how I frightened you when I said something like that to you from my pedestal in Seville? It sounds rather flat without my trombones.

DON JUAN. They tell me it generally sounds flat with them, Commander.

ANA. Oh, do not interrupt with these frivolities, father. Is there nothing in Heaven but contemplation, Juan?

DON JUAN. In the Heaven I seek, no other joy. But there is the work of helping Life in its struggle upward. Think of how it wastes and scatters itself, how it raises up obstacles to itself and destroys itself in its ignorance and blindness. It needs a brain, this irresistible force, lest in its ignorance it should resist itself. What a piece of work is man! says the poet. Yes; but what a blunderer! Here is the highest miracle of organization yet attained by life, the most intensely alive thing that exists, the most conscious of all the organisms; and yet, how wretched are his brains! Stupidity made sordid and cruel by the realities learnt from toil and poverty: Imagination resolved to starve sooner than face these realities, piling up illusions to hide them, and calling itself cleverness, genius! And each accusing the other of its own defect: Stupidity accusing Imagination of folly, and Imagination accusing Stupidity of ignorance: whereas, alas! Stupidity has all the knowledge, and Imagination all the intelligence.

THE DEVIL. And a pretty kettle of fish they make of it between them. Did I not say, when I was arranging that affair of Faust's, that all Man's reason has done for him is to make him beastlier than any beast. One splendid body is worth the brains of a hundred dyspeptic, flatulent philosophers.

DON JUAN. You forget that brainless magnificence of body has been tried. Things immeasurably greater than man in every respect but brain have existed and perished. The megatherium, the icthyosaurus have paced the earth with seven-league steps and hidden the day with cloud vast wings. Where are they now? Fossils in museums, and so few and imperfect at that, that a knuckle bone or a tooth of one of them is prized beyond the lives of a thousand soldiers. These things lived and wanted to live; but for lack of brains they did not know how to carry out their purpose, and so destroyed themselves.

THE DEVIL. And is Man any the less destroying himself for all this boasted brain of his? Have you walked up and down upon the earth lately? I have; and I have examined Man's wonderful inventions. And I tell you that in the arts of life man invents nothing; but in the arts of death he outdoes Nature herself, and produces by chemistry and machinery all the slaughter of plague, pestilence, and famine. The peasant I tempt today eats and drinks what was eaten and drunk by the peasants of ten thousand years ago; and the house he lives in has not altered as much in a thousand centuries as the fashion of a lady's bonnet in a score of weeks. But when he goes out to slay, he carries a marvel of mechanism that lets loose at the touch of his finger all the hidden molecular energies, and leaves the javelin, the arrow, the blowpipe of his fathers far behind. In the arts of peace Man is a bungler. I have seen his cotton factories and the like, with machinery that a greedy dog could have invented if it had wanted money instead of food. I know his clumsy typewriters and bungling locomotives and tedious bicycles: they are toys compared to the Maxim gun, the submarine torpedo boat. There is nothing in Man's industrial machinery but his greed and sloth: his heart is in his weapons. This marvellous force of Life of which you boast is a force of Death: Man measures his strength by his destructiveness. What is his religion? An excuse for hating me. What is his law? An excuse for hanging you. What is his morality? Gentility! an excuse for consuming without producing. What is his art? An excuse for gloating over pictures of slaughter. What are his politics? Either the worship of a despot because a despot can kill, or parliamentary cock-fighting. I spent an evening lately in a certain celebrated legislature, and heard the pot lecturing the kettle for its blackness, and ministers answering questions. When I left I chalked up on the door the old nursery saying "Ask no questions and you will be told no lies." I bought a sixpenny family magazine, and found it full of pictures of young men shooting and stabbing one another. I saw a man die: he was a London bricklayer's laborer with seven children. He left seventeen pounds club money; and his wife spent it all on his funeral and went into the workhouse with the children next day. She would not have spent sevenpence on her children's schooling: the law had to force her to let them be taught gratuitously; but on death she spent all she had. Their imagination glows, their energies rise up at the idea of death, these people: they love it; and the more horrible it is the more they enjoy it. Hell is a place far above their comprehension: they derive their notion of it from two of the greatest fools that ever lived, an Italian and an Englishman. The Italian described it as a place of mud, frost, filth, fire, and venomous serpents: all torture. This ass, when he was not lying about me, was maundering about some woman whom he saw once in the street. The Englishman described me as being expelled from Heaven by cannons and gunpowder; and to this day every Briton believes that the whole of his silly story is in the Bible. What else he says I do not know; for it is all in a long poem which neither I nor anyone else ever succeeded in wading through. It is the same in everything. The highest form of literature is the tragedy, a play in which everybody is murdered at the end. In the old chronicles you read of earthquakes and pestilences, and are told that these shewed the power and majesty of God and the littleness of Man. Nowadays the chronicles describe

battles. In a battle two bodies of men shoot at one another
with bullets and explosive shells until one body runs away,
when the others chase the fugitives on horseback and cut
them to pieces as they fly. And this, the chronicle concludes,
shews the greatness and majesty of empires, and the littleness of the vanquished. Over such battles the people run
about the streets yelling with delight, and egg their Govern-
ments on to spend hundreds of millions of money in the
slaughter, whilst the strongest Ministers dare not spend an
extra penny in the pound against the poverty and pestilence
through which they themselves daily walk. I could give you
a thousand instances; but they all come to the same thing:
the power that governs the earth is not the power of Life but
of Death; and the inner need that has nerved Life to the
effort of organizing itself into the human being is not the
need for higher life but for a more efficient engine of de-
struction. The plague, the famine, the earthquake, the tem-
pest were too spasmodic in their action; the tiger and croco-
dile were too easily satiated and not cruel enough: something more constantly, more ruthlessly, more ingeniously
destructive was needed; and that something was Man, the
inventor of the rack, the stake, the gallows, the electric
chair; of sword and gun and poison gas: above all, of justice,
duty, patriotism, and all the other isms by which even those
who are clever enough to be humanely disposed are per-
suaded to become the most destructive of all the destroyers.

DON JUAN. Pshaw! all this is old. Your weak side, my
diabolic friend, is that you have always been a gull: you take
Man at his own valuation. Nothing would flatter him more
than your opinion of him. He loves to think of himself as
bold and bad. He is neither one nor the other: he is only a
coward. Call him tyrant, murderer, pirate, bully; and he
will adore you, and swagger about with the consciousness of
having the blood of the old sea kings in his veins. Call him
liar and thief; and he will only take an action against you for
libel. But call him coward; and he will go mad with rage: he
will face death to outface that stinging truth. Man gives

every reason for his conduct save one, every excuse for his crimes save one, every plea for his safety save one; and that one is his cowardice. Yet all his civilization is founded on his cowardice, on his abject tameness, which he calls his respectability. There are limits to what a mule or an ass will stand; but Man will suffer himself to be degraded until his vileness becomes so loathsome to his oppressors that they themselves are forced to reform it.

THE DEVIL. Precisely. And these are the creatures in whom you discover what you call a Life Force!

DON JUAN. Yes; for now comes the most surprising part of the whole business.

THE STATUE. Whats that?

DON JUAN. Why, that you can make any of these cowards brave by simply putting an idea into his head.

THE STATUE. Stuff! As an old soldier I admit the cowardice: it's as universal as sea sickness, and matters just as little. But that about putting an idea into a man's head is stuff and nonsense. In a battle all you need to make you fight is a little hot blood and the knowledge that it's more dangerous to lose than to win.

DON JUAN. That is perhaps why battles are so useless. But men never really overcome fear until they imagine they are fighting to further a universal purpose—fighting for an idea, as they call it. Why was the Crusader braver than the pirate? Because he fought, not for himself, but for the Cross. What force was it that met him with a valor as reckless as his own? The force of men who fought, not for themselves, but for Islam. They took Spain from us, though we were fighting for our very hearths and homes; but when we, too, fought for that mighty idea, a Catholic Church, we swept them back to Africa.

THE DEVIL [ironically] What! you a Catholic, Señor Don Juan! A devotee! My congratulations.

THE STATUE [seriously] Come, come! as a soldier, I can listen to nothing against the Church.

DON JUAN. Have no fear, Commander: this idea of a

Catholic Church will survive Islam, will survive the Cross, will survive even that vulgar pageant of incompetent schoolboyish gladiators which you call the Army.

THE STATUE. Juan: you will force me to call you to account for this.

DON JUAN. Useless: I cannot fence. Every idea for which Man will die will be a Catholic idea. When the Spaniard learns at last that he is no better than the Saracen, and his prophet no better than Mahomet, he will arise, more Catholic than ever, and die on a barricade across the filthy slum he starves in, for universal liberty and equality.

THE STATUE. Bosh!

DON JUAN. What you call bosh is the only thing men dare die for. Later on, Liberty will not be Catholic enough: men will die for human perfection, to which they will sacrifice all their liberty gladly.

THE DEVIL. Ay: they will never be at a loss for an excuse for killing one another.

DON JUAN. What of that? It is not death that matters, but the fear of death. It is not killing and dying that degrades us, but base living, and accepting the wages and profits of degradation. Better ten dead men than one live slave or his master. Men shall yet rise up, father against son and brother against brother, and kill one another for the great Catholic idea of abolishing slavery.

THE DEVIL. Yes, when the Liberty and Equality of which you prate shall have made free white Christians cheaper in the labor market than black heathen slaves sold by auction at the block.

DON JUAN. Never fear! the white laborer shall have his turn too. But I am not now defending the illusory forms the great ideas take. I am giving you examples of the fact that this creature Man, who in his own selfish affairs is a coward to the backbone, will fight for an idea like a hero. He may be abject as a citizen; but he is dangerous as a fanatic. He can only be enslaved whilst he is spiritually weak enough to listen to reason. I tell you, gentlemen, if you can shew a man a piece of what he now calls God's work to do, and what he will later on call by many new names, you can make him entirely reckless of the consequences to himself personally.

ANA. Yes: he shirks all his responsibilities, and leaves his wife to grapple with them.

THE STATUE. Well said, daughter. Do not let him talk you out of your common sense.

THE DEVIL. Alas! Señor Commander, now that we have got on to the subject of Woman, he will talk more than ever. However, I confess it is for me the one supremely interesting subject.

DON JUAN. To a woman, Señora, man's duties and responsibilities begin and end with the task of getting bread for her children. To her, Man is only a means to the end of getting children and rearing them.

ANA. Is that your idea of a woman's mind? I call it cynical and disgusting animalism.

DON JUAN. Pardon me, Ana: I said nothing about a woman's whole mind. I spoke of her view of Man as a separate sex. It is no more cynical than her view of herself as above all things a Mother. Sexually, Woman is Nature's contrivance for perpetuating its highest achievement. Sexually, Man is Woman's contrivance for fulfilling Nature's behest in the most economical way. She knows by instinct that far back in the evolutional process she invented him, differentiated him, created him in order to produce something better than the single-sexed process can produce. Whilst he fulfils the purpose for which she made him, he is welcome to his dreams, his follies, his ideals, his heroisms, provided that the keystone of them all is the worship of woman, of motherhood, of the family, of the hearth. But how rash and dangerous it was to invent a separate creature whose sole function was her own impregnation! For mark what has happened. First, Man has multiplied on her hands until there are as many men as women; so that she has been unable to employ for her purposes more than a fraction of the immense energy she has left at his disposal by saving him the exhausting labor of gestation. This superfluous energy has gone to his brain and to his muscle. He has become too strong to be controlled by her bodily, and too imaginative and mentally vigorous to be content with mere self-reproduction. He has created civilization without consulting her, taking her domestic labor for granted as the foundation of it.

ANA. That is true, at all events.

THE DEVIL. Yes; and this civilization! what is it, after all?

DON JUAN. After all, an excellent peg to hang your cynical commonplaces on; but before all, it is an attempt on Man's part to make himself something more than the mere instrument of Woman's purpose. So far, the result of Life's continual effort not only to maintain itself, but to achieve higher and higher organization and completer self-consciousness, is only, at best, a doubtful campaign between its forces and those of Death and Degeneration. The battles in this campaign are mere blunders, mostly won, like actual military battles, in spite of the commanders.

THE STATUE. That is a dig at me. No matter: go on, go on.

DON JUAN. It is a dig at a much higher power than you, Commander. Still, you must have noticed in your profession that even a stupid general can win battles when the enemy's general is a little stupider.

THE STATUE [*very seriously*] Most true, Juan, most true. Some donkeys have amazing luck.

DON JUAN. Well, the Life Force is stupid; but it is not so stupid as the forces of Death and Degeneration. Besides, these are in its pay all the time. And so Life wins, after a fashion. What mere copiousness of fecundity can supply and mere greed preserve, we possess. The survival of whatever form of civilization can produce the best rifle and the best fed riflemen is assured.

THE DEVIL. Exactly! the survival, not of the most effective means of Life but of the most effective means of Death. You always come back to my point, in spite of your wrigglings and evasions and sophistries, not to mention the intolerable length of your speeches.

DON JUAN. Oh, come! who began making long speeches? However, if I overtax your intellect, you can leave us and seek the society of love and beauty and the rest of your favorite boredoms.

THE DEVIL [*much offended*] This is not fair, Don Juan, and not civil. I am also on the intellectual plane. Nobody can appreciate it more than I do. I am arguing fairly with you, and, I think, successfully refuting you. Let us go on for another hour if you like.

DON JUAN. Good: let us.

THE STATUE. Not that I see any prospect of your coming to any point in particular, Juan. Still, since in this place, instead of merely killing time we have to kill eternity, go ahead by all means.

DON JUAN [*somewhat impatiently*] My point, you marble-headed old masterpiece, is only a step ahead of you. Are we agreed that Life is a force which has made innumerable experiments in organizing itself; that the mammoth and the man, the mouse and the megatherium, the flies and the fleas and the Fathers of the Church, are all more or less successful attempts to build up that raw force into higher and higher individuals, the ideal individual being omnipotent, omniscient, infallible, and withal completely, unilludedly self-conscious: in short, a god?

THE DEVIL. I agree, for the sake of argument.

THE STATUE. I agree, for the sake of avoiding argument.

ANA. I most emphatically disagree as regards the Fathers of the Church; and I must beg you not to drag them into the argument.

DON JUAN. I did so purely for the sake of alliteration, Ana; and I shall make no further allusion to them. And now, since we are, with that exception, agreed so far, will you not agree with me further that Life has not measured the success of its attempts at godhead by the beauty or bodily perfection of the result, since in both these respects the birds, as our friend Aristophanes long ago pointed out, are so extraordinarily superior, with their power of flight and their lovely plumage, and, may I add, the touching poetry of their loves and nestings, that it is inconceivable that Life, having once produced them, should, if love and beauty were her object, start off on another line and labor at the clumsy elephant and the hideous ape, whose grandchildren we are?

ANA. Aristophanes was a heathen; and you, Juan, I am afraid, are very little better.

THE DEVIL. You conclude, then, that Life was driving at clumsiness and ugliness?

DON JUAN. No, perverse devil that you are, a thousand times no. Life was driving at brains—at its darling object: an organ by which it can attain not only self-consciousness but self-understanding.

THE STATUE. This is metaphysics, Juan. Why the devil should—[*to The Devil*] I beg your pardon.

THE DEVIL. Pray dont mention it. I have always regarded the use of my name to secure additional emphasis as a high compliment to me. It is quite at your service, Commander.

THE STATUE. Thank you: thats very good of you. Even in heaven, I never quite got out of my old military habits of speech. What I was going to ask Juan was why Life should bother itself about getting a brain. Why should it want to understand itself? Why not be content to enjoy itself?

DON JUAN. Without a brain, Commander, you would enjoy yourself without knowing it, and so lose all the fun.

THE STATUE. True, most true. But I am quite content with brain enough to know that I'm enjoying myself. I dont want to understand why. In fact, I'd rather not. My experience is that one's pleasures dont bear thinking about.

DON JUAN. That is why intellect is so unpopular. But to Life, the force behind the Man, intellect is a necessity, because without it he blunders into death. Just as Life, after ages of struggle, evolved that wonderful bodily organ the eye, so that the living organism could see where it was going and what was coming to help or threaten it, and thus avoid a thousand dangers that formerly slew it, so it is evolving today a mind's eye that shall see, not the physical world, but the purpose of Life, and thereby enable the individual to work for that purpose instead of thwarting and baffling it by setting up shortsighted personal aims as at present. Even as it is, only one sort of man has ever been happy, has ever been universally respected among all the conflicts of interests and illusions.

THE STATUE. You mean the military man.

DON JUAN. Commander: I do n o t mean the military man. When the military man approaches, the world locks up its spoons and packs off its womankind. No: I sing, not arms and the hero, but the philosophic man: he who seeks in contemplation to discover the inner will of the world, in invention to discover the means of fulfilling that will, and in action to do that will by the so-discovered means. Of all other sorts of men I declare myself tired. They are tedious failures. When I was on earth, professors of all sorts prowled round me feeling for an unhealthy spot in me on which they could fasten. The doctors of medicine bade me consider what I must do to save my body, and offered me quack cures for imaginary diseases. I replied that I was not a hypochondriac; so they called me Ignoramus and went their way. The doctors of divinity bade me consider what I must do to save my soul; but I was not a spiritual hypochondriac any more than a bodily one, and would not trouble myself about that either; so they called me Atheist and went their way. After them came the politician, who said there was only one purpose in nature, and that was to get him into parliament. I told him I did not care whether he got into parliament or not; so he called me Mugwump and went his way. Then came the romantic man, the Artist, with his love songs and his paintings and his poems; and with him I had great delight for many years, and some profit; for I cultivated my senses for his sake; and his songs taught me to hear better, his paintings to see better, and his poems to feel more deeply. But he led me at last into the worship of Woman.

ANA. Juan!

DON JUAN. Yes: I came to believe that in her voice was all the music of the song, in her face all the beauty of the painting, and in her soul all the emotion of the poem.

ANA. And you were disappointed, I suppose. Well, was it her fault that you attributed all these perfections to her?

DON JUAN. Yes, partly. For with a wonderful instinctive cunning, she kept silent and allowed me to glorify her: to mistake my own visions, thoughts, and feelings for hers. Now my friend the romantic man was often too poor or too timid to approach those women who were beautiful or refined enough to seem to realize his ideal; and so he went to his grave believing in his dream. But I was more favored by nature and circumstance. I was of noble birth and rich; and when my person did not please, my conversation flattered, though I generally found myself fortunate in both.

THE STATUE. Coxcomb!

DON JUAN. Yes; but even my coxcombry pleased. Well, I found that when I had touched a woman's imagination, she would allow me to persuade myself that she loved me; but when my suit was granted she never said "I am happy: my love is satisfied": she always said, first, "At last, the barriers are down," and second, "When will you come again?"

ANA. That is exactly what men say.

DON JUAN. I protest I never said it. But all women say it. Well, these two speeches always alarmed me; for the first meant that the lady's impulse had been solely to throw down my fortifications and gain my citadel; and the second openly announced that henceforth she regarded me as her property, and counted my time as already wholly at her disposal.

THE DEVIL. That is where your want of heart came in.

THE STATUE [*shaking his head*] You shouldnt repeat what a woman says, Juan.

ANA [*severely*] It should be sacred to you.

THE STATUE. Still, they certainly do say it. I never minded the barriers; but there was always a slight shock about the other, unless one was very hard hit indeed.

DON JUAN. Then the lady, who had been happy and idle enough before, became anxious, preoccupied with me, always intriguing, conspiring, pursuing, watching, waiting, bent wholly on making sure of her prey: I being the prey, you understand. Now this was not what I had bargained for. It may have been very proper and very natural; but it was not music, painting, poetry, and joy incarnated in a beautiful woman. I ran away from it. I ran away from it very often: in fact I became famous for running away from it.

ANA. Infamous, you mean.

DON JUAN. I did not run away from you. Do you blame me for running away from the others?

ANA. Nonsense, man. You are talking to a woman of 77 now. If you had had the chance, you would have run away from me too—if I had let you. You would not have found it so easy with me as with some of the others. If men will not be faithful to their home and their duties, they must be made to be. I daresay you all want to marry lovely incarnations of music and painting and poetry. Well, you cant have them, because they dont exist. If flesh and blood is not good enough for you you must go without: thats all. Women have to put up with flesh-and-blood husbands—and little enough of that too, sometimes; and you will have to put up with flesh-and-blood wives. [*The Devil looks dubious. The Statue makes a wry face*]. I see you dont like that, any of you; but it's true, for all that; so if you dont like it you can lump it.

DON JUAN. My dear lady, you have put my whole case against romance into a few sentences. That is just why I turned my back on the romantic man with the artist nature, as he called his infatuation. I thanked him for teaching me to use my eyes and ears; but I told him that his beauty worshipping and happiness hunting and woman idealizing was not worth a dump as a philosophy of life; so he called me Philistine and went his way.

ANA. It seems that Woman taught you something, too, with all her defects.

DON JUAN. She did more: she interpreted all the other teaching for me. Ah, my friends, when the barriers were down for the first time, what an astounding illumination! I had been prepared for infatuation, for intoxication, for all the illusions of love's young dream; and lo! never was my perception clearer, nor my criticism more ruthless. The most jealous rival of my mistress never saw every blemish in her more keenly than I. I was not duped: I took her without chloroform.

ANA. But you did take her.

DON JUAN. That was the revelation. Up to that moment I had never lost the sense of being my own master; never consciously taken a single step until my reason had examined and approved it. I had come to believe that I was a purely rational creature: a thinker! I said, with the foolish philosopher, "I think; therefore I am." It was Woman who taught me to say "I am; therefore I think." And also "I would think more; therefore I must be more."

THE STATUE. This is extremely abstract and metaphysical, Juan. If you would stick to the concrete, and put your discoveries in the form of entertaining anecdotes about your adventures with women, your conversation would be easier to follow.

DON JUAN. Bah! what need I add? Do you not understand that when I stood face to face with Woman, every fibre in my clear critical brain warned me to spare her and save myself. My morals said No. My conscience said No. My chivalry and pity for her said No. My prudent regard for myself said No. My ear, practised on a thousand songs and symphonies; my eye, exercised on a thousand paintings; tore her voice, her features, her color to shreds. I caught all those tell-tale resemblances to her father and mother by which I knew what she would be like in thirty years' time.

I noted the gleam of gold from a dead tooth in the laughing mouth: I made curious observations of the strange odors of the chemistry of the nerves. The visions of my romantic reveries, in which I had trod the plains of heaven with a deathless, ageless creature of coral and ivory, deserted me in that supreme hour. I remembered them and desperately strove to recover their illusion; but they now seemed the emptiest of inventions: my judgment was not to be corrupted: my brain still said No on every issue. And whilst I was in the act of framing my excuse to the lady, Life seized me and threw me into her arms as a sailor throws a scrap of fish into the mouth of a seabird.

THE STATUE. You might as well have gone without thinking such a lot about it, Juan. You are like all the clever men: you have more brains than is good for you.

THE DEVIL. And were you not the happier for the experience, Señor Don Juan?

DON JUAN. The happier, no: the wiser, yes. That moment introduced me for the first time to myself, and, through myself, to the world. I saw then how useless it is to attempt to impose conditions on the irresistible force of Life; to preach prudence, careful selection, virtue, honor, chastity—

ANA. Don Juan: a word against chastity is an insult to me.

DON JUAN. I say nothing against your chastity, Señora, since it took the form of a husband and twelve children. What more could you have done had you been the most abandoned of women?

ANA. I could have had twelve husbands and no children: thats what I could have done, Juan. And let me tell you that that would have made all the difference to the earth which I replenished.

THE STATUE. Bravo Ana! Juan: you are floored, quelled, annihilated.

DON JUAN. No; for though that difference is the true essential difference—Doña Ana has, I admit, gone straight to the real point—yet it is not a difference of love or chastity, or even constancy; for twelve children by twelve different husbands would have replenished the earth perhaps more effectively. Suppose my friend Ottavio had died when you were thirty, you would never have remained a widow: you were too beautiful. Suppose the successor of Ottavio had died when you were forty, you would still have been irresistible; and a woman who marries twice marries three times if she becomes free to do so. Twelve lawful children borne by one highly respectable lady to three different fathers is not impossible nor condemned by public opinion. That such a lady may be more law abiding than the poor girl whom we used to spurn into the gutter for bearing one unlawful infant is no doubt true; but dare you say she is less self-indulgent?

ANA. She is more virtuous: that is enough for me.

DON JUAN. In that case, what is virtue but the Trade Unionism of the married? Let us face the facts, dear Ana. The Life Force respects marriage only because marriage is a contrivance of its own to secure the greatest number of children and the closest care of them. For honor, chastity, and all the rest of your moral figments it cares not a rap. Marriage is the most licentious of human institutions—

ANA. Juan!

THE STATUE [*protesting*] Really!—

DON JUAN [*determinedly*] I say the most licentious of human institutions: that is the secret of its popularity. And a woman seeking a husband is the most unscrupulous of all the beasts of prey. The confusion of marriage with morality has done more to destroy the conscience of the human race than any other single error. Come, Ana! do not look shocked: you know better than any of us that marriage is a mantrap baited with simulated accomplishments and delusive idealizations. When your sainted mother, by dint of scoldings and punishments, forced you to learn how to play half a dozen pieces on the spinet—which she hated as much as you did—had she any other purpose than to delude your suitors into the belief that your husband would have in his home an angel who would fill it with melody, or at least play him to sleep after dinner? You married my friend Ottavio:

well, did you ever open the spinet from the hour when the Church united him to you?

ANA. You are a fool, Juan. A young married woman has something else to do than sit at the spinet without any support for her back; so she gets out of the habit of playing.

DON JUAN. Not if she loves music. No: believe me, she only throws away the bait when the bird is in the net.

ANA [*bitterly*] And men, I suppose, never throw off the mask when their bird is in the net. The husband never becomes negligent, selfish, brutal—oh, never!

DON JUAN. What do these recriminations prove, Ana? Only that the hero is as gross an imposture as the heroine.

ANA. It is all nonsense: most marriages are perfectly comfortable.

DON JUAN. "Perfectly" is a strong expression, Ana. What you mean is that sensible people make the best of one another. Send me to the galleys and chain me to the felon whose number happens to be next before mine; and I must accept the inevitable and make the best of the companionship. Many such companionships, they tell me, are touchingly affectionate; and most are at least tolerably friendly. But that does not make a chain a desirable ornament nor the galleys an abode of bliss. Those who talk most about the blessings of marriage and the constancy of its vows are the very people who declare that if the chain were broken and the prisoners left free to choose, the whole social fabric would fly asunder. You cannot have the argument both ways. If the prisoner is happy, why lock him in? If he is not, why pretend that he is?

ANA. At all events, let me take an old woman's privilege again, and tell you flatly that marriage peoples the world and debauchery does not.

DON JUAN. How if a time come when this shall cease to be true? Do you not know that where there is a will there is a way? that whatever Man really wishes to do he will finally discover a means of doing? Well, you have done your best, you virtuous ladies, and others of your way of thinking, to bend Man's mind wholly towards honorable love as the highest good, and to understand by honorable love, romance and beauty and happiness in the possession of beautiful, refined, delicate, affectionate women. You have taught women to value their own youth, health, shapeliness, and refinement above all things. Well, what place have squalling babies and household cares in this exquisite paradise of the senses and emotions? Is it not the inevitable end of it all that the human will shall say to the human brain: Invent me a means by which I can have love, beauty, romance, emotion, passion, without their wretched penalties, their expenses, their worries, their trials, their illnesses and agonies and risks of death, their retinue of servants and nurses and doctors and schoolmasters.

THE DEVIL. All this, Señor Don Juan, is realized here in my realm.

DON JUAN. Yes, at the cost of death. Man will not take it at that price: he demands the romantic delights of your hell whilst he is still on earth. Well, the means will be found: the brain will not fail when the will is in earnest. The day is coming when great nations will find their numbers dwindling from census to census; when the six roomed villa will rise in price above the family mansion; when the viciously reckless poor and the stupidly pious rich will delay the extinction of the race only by degrading it; whilst the boldly prudent, the thriftily selfish and ambitious, the imaginative and poetic, the lovers of money and solid comfort, the worshippers of success, of art, and of love, will all oppose to the Force of Life the device of sterility.

THE STATUE. That is all very eloquent, my young friend; but if you had lived to Ana's age, or even to mine, you would have learned that the people who get rid of the fear of poverty and children and all the other family troubles, and devote themselves to having a good time of it, only leave their minds free for the fear of old age and ugliness and impotence and death. The childless laborer is more tormented by his wife's idleness and her constant demands for amusement and distraction than he could be by twenty children; and his wife is more wretched than he. I have had my share of vanity; for as a young man I was admired by women; and as a statue I am praised by art critics. But I confess that had I found nothing to do in the world but wallow in these delights I should have cut my throat. When I married Ana's mother —or perhaps, to be strictly correct, I should rather say when I at last gave in and allowed Ana's mother to marry me—I knew that I was planting thorns in my pillow, and that marriage for me, a swaggering young officer thitherto unvanquished, meant defeat and capture.

ANA [*scandalized*] Father!

THE STATUE. I am sorry to shock you, my love; but since Juan has stripped every rag of decency from the discussion I may as well tell the frozen truth.

ANA. Hmf! I suppose I was one of the thorns.

THE STATUE. By no means: you were often a rose. You see, your mother had most of the trouble you gave.

DON JUAN. Then may I ask, Commander, why you have left Heaven to come here and wallow, as you express it, in sentimental beatitudes which you confess would once have driven you to cut your throat?

THE STATUE [*struck by this*] Egad, thats true.

THE DEVIL [*alarmed*] What! You are going back from your word! [*To Don Juan*] And all your philosophizing has been nothing but a mask for proselytizing! [*To the Statue*] Have you forgotten already the hideous dulness from which I am offering you a refuge here? [*To Don Juan*] And does your demonstration of the approaching sterilization and extinction of mankind lead to anything better than making the most of those pleasures of art and love which you yourself admit refined you, elevated you, developed you?

DON JUAN. I never demonstrated the extinction of mankind. Life cannot will its own extinction either in its blind amorphous state or in any of the forms into which it has organized itself. I had not finished when His Excellency interrupted me.

THE STATUE. I begin to doubt whether you ever will finish, my friend. You are extremely fond of hearing yourself talk.

DON JUAN. True; but since you have endured so much, you may as well endure to the end. Long before this sterilization which I described becomes more than a clearly foreseen possibility, the reaction will begin. The great central purpose of breeding the race: ay, breeding it to heights now deemed superhuman: that purpose which is now hidden in a mephitic cloud of love and romance and prudery and fastidiousness, will break through into clear sunlight as a purpose no longer to be confused with the gratification of personal fancies, the impossible realization of boys' and girls' dreams of bliss, or the need of older people for companionship or money. The plain-spoken marriage services of the vernacular Churches will no longer be abbreviated and half suppressed as indelicate. The sober decency, earnestness, and authority of their declaration of the real purpose of marriage will be honored and accepted, whilst their romantic vowings and pledgings and until-death-do-us-partings and the like will be expunged as unbearable frivolities. Do my sex the justice to admit, Señora, that we have always recognized that the sex relation is not a personal or friendly relation at all.

ANA. Not a personal or friendly relation! What relation is more personal? more sacred? more holy?

DON JUAN. Sacred and holy, if you like, Ana, but not personally friendly. Your relation to God is sacred and holy: dare you call it personally friendly? In the sex relation the universal creative energy, of which the parties are both the helpless agents, over-rides and sweeps away all personal considerations, and dispenses with all personal relations. The pair may be utter strangers to one another, speaking different languages, differing in race and color, in age and disposition, with no bond between them but a possibility of that fecundity for the sake of which the Life Force throws them into one another's arms at the exchange of a glance. Do we not recognize this by allowing marriages to be made by parents without consulting the woman? Have you not often expressed your disgust at the immorality of the English nation, in which women and men of noble birth become acquainted and court each other like peasants? And how much does even the peasant know of his bride or she of him before he engages himself? Why, you would not make a man your lawyer or your family doctor on so slight an acquaintance as you would fall in love with and marry him!

ANA. Yes, Juan: we know the libertine's philosophy. Always ignore the consequences to the woman.

DON JUAN. The consequences, yes: they justify her fierce grip of the man. But surely you do not call that attachment a sentimental one. As well call the policeman's attachment to his prisoner a love relation.

ANA. You see you have to confess that marriage is necessary, though, according to you, love is the slightest of all human relations.

DON JUAN. How do you know that it is not the greatest of all human relations? far too great to be a personal matter. Could your father have served his country if he had refused to kill any enemy of Spain unless he personally hated him? Can a woman serve her country if she refuses to marry any man she does not personally love? You know it is not so: the woman of noble birth marries as the man of noble birth fights, on political and family grounds, not on personal ones.

THE STATUE [impressed] A very clever point that, Juan: I must think it over. You are really full of ideas. How did you come to think of this one?

DON JUAN. I learnt it by experience. When I was on earth, and made those proposals to ladies which, though universally condemned, have made me so interesting a hero of legend, I was not infrequently met in some such way as this. The lady would say that she would countenance my advances, provided they were honorable. On inquiring what that proviso meant, I found that it meant that I proposed to get possession of her property if she had any, or to undertake her support for life if she had not; that I desired her continual companionship, counsel, and conversation to the end of my days, and would take a most solemn oath to be always enraptured by them: above all, that I would turn my back on all other women for ever for her sake. I did not object to these conditions because they were exorbitant and inhuman: it was their extraordinary irrelevance that prostrated me. I invariably replied with perfect frankness that I had never dreamt of any of these things; that unless the lady's character and intellect were equal or superior to my own, her conversation must degrade and her counsel mislead me; that her constant companionship might, for all I knew, become intolerably tedious to me; that I could not answer for my feelings for a week in advance, much less to the end of my life; that to cut me off from all natural and unconstrained intercourse with half my fellowcreatures would narrow and warp me if I submitted to it, and, if not, would bring me under the curse of clandestinity; that, finally, my proposals to her were wholly unconnected with any of these matters, and were the outcome of a perfectly simple impulse of my manhood towards her womanhood.

ANA. You mean that it was an immoral impulse.

DON JUAN. Nature, my dear lady, is what you call immoral. I blush for it; but I cannot help it. Nature is a pandar, Time a wrecker, and Death a murderer. I have always preferred to stand up to those facts and build institutions on their recognition. You prefer to propitiate the three devils by proclaiming their chastity, their thrift, and their loving kindness; and to base your institutions on these flatteries. Is it any wonder that the institutions do not work smoothly?

THE STATUE. What used the ladies to say, Juan?

DON JUAN. Oh, come! Confidence for confidence. First tell me what you used to say to the ladies.

THE STATUE. I! Oh, I swore that I would be faithful to the death; that I should die if they refused me; that no woman could ever be to me what she was—

ANA. She! Who?

THE STATUE. Whoever it happened to be at the time, my

dear. I had certain things I always said. One of them was that even when I was eighty, one white hair of the woman I loved would make me tremble more than the thickest gold tress from the most beautiful young head. Another was that I could not bear the thought of anyone else being the mother of my children.

DON JUAN [*revolted*] You old rascal!

THE STATUE [*stoutly*] Not a bit; for I really believed it with all my soul at the moment, I had a heart: not like you. And it was this sincerity that made me successful.

DON JUAN. Sincerity! To be fool enough to believe a ramping, stamping, thumping lie: that is what you call sincerity! To be so greedy for a woman that you deceive yourself in your eagerness to deceive her: sincerity, you call it!

THE STATUE. Oh, damn your sophistries! I was a man in love, not a lawyer. And the women loved me for it, bless them!

DON JUAN. They made you think so. What will you say when I tell you that though I played the lawyer so callously, they made me think so too? I also had my moments of infatuation in which I gushed nonsense and believed it. Sometimes the desire to give pleasure by saying beautiful things so rose in me on the flood of emotion that I said them recklessly. At other times I argued against myself with a devilish coldness that drew tears. But I found it just as hard to escape when I was cruel as when I was kind. When the lady's instinct was set on me, there was nothing for it but lifelong servitude or flight.

ANA. You dare boast, before me and my father, that every woman found you irresistible.

DON JUAN. Am I boasting? It seems to me that I cut the most pitiable of figures. Besides, I said "when the lady's instinct was set on me." It was not always so; and then, heavens! what transports of virtuous indignation! what overwhelming defiance to the dastardly seducer! what scenes of Imogen and Iachimo!

ANA. I made no scenes. I simply called my father.

DON JUAN. And he came, sword in hand, to vindicate outraged honor and morality by murdering me.

THE STATUE. Murdering! What do you mean? Did I kill you or did you kill me?

DON JUAN. Which of us was the better fencer?

THE STATUE. I was.

DON JUAN. Of course you were. And yet you, the hero of those scandalous adventures you have just been relating to us, you had the effrontery to pose as the avenger of outraged morality and condemn me to death! You would have slain me but for an accident.

THE STATUE. I was expected to, Juan. That is how things were arranged on earth. I was not a social reformer; and I always did what it was customary for a gentleman to do.

DON JUAN. That may account for your attacking me, but not for the revolting hypocrisy of your subsequent proceedings as a statue.

THE STATUE. That all came of my going to Heaven.

THE DEVIL. I still fail to see, Señor Don Juan, that these episodes in your earthly career and in that of the Señor Commander in any way discredit my view of life. Here, I repeat, you have all that you sought without anything that you shrank from.

DON JUAN. On the contrary, here I have everything that disappointed me without anything that I have not already tried and found wanting. I tell you that as long as I can conceive something better than myself I cannot be easy unless I am striving to bring it into existence or clearing the way for it. That is the law of my life. That is the working within me of Life's incessant aspiration to higher organization, wider, deeper, intenser self-consciousness, and clearer self-understanding. It was the supremacy of this purpose that reduced love for me to the mere pleasure of a moment, art for me to the mere schooling of my faculties, religion for me to a mere excuse for laziness, since it had set up a God who looked at the world and saw that it was good, against the instinct in me that looked through my eyes at the world and saw that it could be improved. I tell you that in the pursuit of my own pleasure, my own health, my own fortune, I have never known happiness. It was not love for Woman that delivered me into her hands: it was fatigue, exhaustion. When I was a child, and bruised my head against a stone, I ran to the nearest woman and cried away my pain against her apron. When I grew up, and bruised my soul against the brutalities and stupidities with which I had to strive, I did again just what I had done as a child. I have enjoyed, too, my rests, my recuperations, my breathing times, my very prostrations after strife; but rather would I be dragged through all the circles of the foolish Italian's Inferno than through the pleasures of Europe. That is what has made this place of eternal pleasures so deadly to me. It is the absence of this instinct in you that makes you that strange monster called a Devil. It is the success with which you have diverted the attention of men from their real purpose, which in one degree or another is the same as mine, to yours, that has earned you the name of The Tempter. It is the fact that they are doing your will, or rather drifting with your want of will, instead of doing their own, that makes them the uncomfortable, false, restless, artificial, petulant, wretched creatures they are.

THE DEVIL [*mortified*] Señor Don Juan: you are uncivil to my friends.

DON JUAN. Pooh! why should I be civil to them or to you? In this Palace of Lies a truth or two will not hurt you. Your friends are all the dullest dogs I know. They are not beautiful: they are only decorated. They are not clean: they are only shaved and starched. They are not dignified: they are only fashionably dressed. They are not educated: they are only college passmen. They are not religious: they are only pewrenters. They are not moral: they are only conventional. They are not virtuous: they are only cowardly. They are not even vicious: they are only "frail." They are not artistic: they are only lascivious. They are not prosperous: they are only rich. They are not loyal, they are only servile; not dutiful, only sheepish; not public spirited, only patriotic; not courageous, only quarrelsome; not determined, only obstinate; not masterful, only domineering; not self-controlled, only obtuse; not self-respecting, only vain; not kind, only sentimental; not social, only gregarious; not considerate, only polite; not intelligent, only opinionated; not progressive, only factious; not imaginative, only superstitious; not just, only vindictive; not generous, only propitiatory; not disciplined, only cowed; and not truthful at all: liars every one of them, to the very backbone of their souls.

THE STATUE. Your flow of words is simply amazing, Juan. How I wish I could have talked like that to my soldiers.

THE DEVIL. It is mere talk, though. It has all been said before; but what change has it ever made? What notice has the world ever taken of it?

DON JUAN. Yes, it is mere talk. But why is it mere talk? Because, my friend, beauty, purity, respectability, religion, morality, art, patriotism, bravery, and the rest are nothing but words which I or anyone else can turn inside out like a glove. Were they realities, you would have to plead guilty to my indictment; but fortunately for your self-respect, my diabolical friend, they are not realities. As you say, they are mere words, useful for duping barbarians into adopting civilization, or the civilized poor into submitting to be robbed and enslaved. That is the family secret of the governing caste; and if we who are of that caste aimed at more Life for the world instead of at more power and luxury for our miserable selves, that secret would make us great. Now, since I, being a nobleman, am in the secret too, think how tedious to me must be your unending cant about all these moralistic figments, and how squalidly disastrous your sacrifice of your lives to them! If you even believed in your moral game enough to play it fairly, it would be interesting to watch; but you dont: you cheat at every trick; and if your opponent outcheats you, you upset the table and try to murder him.

THE DEVIL. On earth there may be some truth in this, because the people are uneducated and cannot appreciate my religion of love and beauty; but here—

DON JUAN. Oh yes: I know. Here there is nothing but love and beauty. Ugh! it is like sitting for all eternity at the first act of a fashionable play, before the complications begin. Never in my worst moments of superstitious terror on earth did I dream that Hell was so horrible. I live, like a hair-dresser, in the continual contemplation of beauty, toying with silken tresses. I breathe an atmosphere of sweetness, like a confectioner's shopboy. Commander: are there any beautiful women in Heaven?

THE STATUE. None. Absolutely none. All dowdies. Not two pennorth of jewellery among a dozen of them. They might be men of fifty.

DON JUAN. I am impatient to get there. Is the word beauty ever mentioned; and are there any artistic people?

THE STATUE. I give you my word they wont admire a fine statue even when it walks past them.

DON JUAN. I go.

THE DEVIL. Don Juan: shall I be frank with you?

DON JUAN. Were you not so before?

THE DEVIL. As far as I went, yes. But I will now go further, and confess to you that men get tired of everything, of heaven no less than of hell; and that all history is nothing but a record of the oscillations of the world between these two extremes. An epoch is but a swing of the pendulum; and each generation thinks the world is progressing because it is always moving. But when you are as old as I am; when you have a thousand times wearied of heaven, like myself and the Commander, and a thousand times wearied of hell, as you are wearied now, you will no longer imagine that every swing from heaven to hell is an emancipation, every swing from hell to heaven an evolution. Where you now see reform, progress, fulfilment of upward tendency, continual ascent by Man on the stepping stones of his dead selves to higher things, you will see nothing but an infinite comedy of illusion. You will discover the profound truth of the saying of my friend Koheleth, that there is nothing new under the sun. Vanitas vanitatum—

DON JUAN [*out of all patience*] By Heaven, this is worse than your cant about love and beauty. Clever dolt that you are, is a man no better than a worm, or a dog than a wolf, because he gets tired of everything? Shall he give up eating because he destroys his appetite in the act of gratifying it? Is a field idle when it is fallow? Can the Commander expend his hellish energy here without accumulating heavenly energy for his next term of blessedness? Granted that the great Life Force has hit on the device of the clockmaker's pendulum, and uses the earth for its bob; that the history of each oscillation, which seems so novel to us the actors, is but the history of the last oscillation repeated; nay more, that in the unthinkable infinitude of time the sun throws off the earth and catches it again a thousand times as a circus rider throws up a ball, and that our agelong epochs are but the moments between the toss and the catch, has the colossal mechanism no purpose?

THE DEVIL. None, my friend. You think, because you have a purpose, Nature must have one. You might as well expect it to have fingers and toes because you have them.

DON JUAN. But I should not have them if they served no purpose. And I, my friend, am as much a part of Nature as my own finger is a part of me. If my finger is the organ by which I grasp the sword and the mandoline, my brain is the organ by which Nature strives to understand itself. My dog's brain serves only my dog's purposes; but my own brain labors at a knowledge which does nothing for me personally but make my body bitter to me and my decay and death a calamity. Were I not possessed with a purpose beyond my own I had better be a ploughman than a philosopher; for the ploughman lives as long as the philosopher, eats more, sleeps better, and rejoices in the wife of his bosom with less misgiving. This is because the philosopher is in the grip of the Life Force. This Life Force says to him "I have done a thousand wonderful things unconsciously by merely willing to live and following the line of least resistance: now I want to know myself and my destination, and choose my path; so I have made a special brain—a philosopher's brain—to grasp this knowledge for me as the husbandman's hand grasps the plough for me. And this" says the Life Force to the philosopher "must thou strive to do for me until thou diest, when I will make another brain and another philosopher to carry on the work."

THE DEVIL. What is the use of knowing?

DON JUAN. Why, to be able to choose the line of greatest advantage instead of yielding in the direction of the least resistance. Does a ship sail to its destination no better than a log drifts nowhither? The philosopher is Nature's pilot. And there you have our difference: to be in hell is to drift; to be in heaven is to steer.

THE DEVIL. On the rocks, most likely.

DON JUAN. Pooh! which ship goes oftenest on the rocks or to the bottom? the drifting ship or the ship with a pilot on board?

THE DEVIL. Well, well, go your way, Señor Don Juan. I prefer to be my own master and not the tool of any blundering universal force. I know that beauty is good to look at; that music is good to hear; that love is good to feel; and that they are all good to think about and talk about. I know that to be well exercised in these sensations, emotions, and studies is to be a refined and cultivated being. Whatever they may say of me in churches on earth, I know that it is universally admitted in good society that the Prince of Darkness is a gentleman; and that is enough for me. As to your Life Force, which you think irresistible, it is the most resistible thing in the world for a person of any character. But if you are naturally vulgar and credulous, as all reformers are, it will thrust you first into religion, where you will sprinkle water on babies to save their souls from me; then it will drive you from religion into science, where you will snatch the babies from the water sprinkling and inoculate them with disease to save them from catching it accidentally; then you will take to politics, where you will become the catspaw of corrupt functionaries and the henchman of ambitious humbugs; and the end will be despair and decrepitude, broken nerve and shattered hopes, vain regrets for that worst and silliest of wastes and sacrifices, the waste and sacrifice of the power of enjoyment: in a word, the punishment of the fool who pursues the better before he has secured the good.

DON JUAN. But at least I shall not be bored. The service of the Life Force has that advantage, at all events. So fare you well, Señor Satan.

THE DEVIL [*amiably*] Fare you well, Don Juan. I shall often think of our interesting chats about things in general. I wish you every happiness: Heaven, as I said before, suits some people. But if you should change your mind, do not forget that the gates are always open here to the repentant prodigal. If you feel at any time that warmth of heart, sincere unforced affection, innocent enjoyment, and warm, breathing, palpitating reality—

DON JUAN. Why not say flesh and blood at once, though we have left those two greasy commonplaces behind us?

THE DEVIL [*angrily*] You throw my friendly farewell back in my teeth, then, Don Juan?

DON JUAN. By no means. But though there is much to be learnt from a cynical devil, I really cannot stand a sentimental one. Señor Commander: you know the way to the frontier of hell and heaven. Be good enough to direct me.

THE STATUE. Oh, the frontier is only the difference between two ways of looking at things. Any road will take you across it if you really want to get there.

DON JUAN. Good. [*Saluting Doña Ana*] Señora: your servant.

ANA. But I am going with you.

DON JUAN. I can find my own way to heaven, Ana; not yours [*he vanishes*].

ANA. How annoying!

THE STATUE [*calling after him*] Bon voyage, Juan! [*He wafts a final blast of his great rolling chords after him as a parting salute. A faint echo of the first ghostly melody comes back in acknowledgment*]. Ah! there he goes. [*Puffing a long breath out through his lips*] Whew! How he does talk! Theyll never stand it in heaven.

THE DEVIL [*gloomily*] His going is a political defeat. I cannot keep these Life Worshippers: they all go. This is the greatest loss I have had since that Dutch painter went: a fellow who would paint a hag of 70 with as much enjoyment as a Venus of 20.

THE STATUE. I remember: he came to heaven. Rembrandt.

THE DEVIL. Ay, Rembrandt. There is something unnatural about these fellows. Do not listen to their gospel, Señor Commander: it is dangerous. Beware of the pursuit of the Superhuman: it leads to an indiscriminate contempt for the Human. To a man, horses and dogs and cats are mere species, outside the moral world. Well, to the Superman, men and women are a mere species too, also outside the moral world. This Don Juan was kind to women and courteous to men as your daughter here was kind to her pet cats and dogs; but such kindness is a denial of the exclusively human character of the soul.

THE STATUE. And who the deuce is the Superman?

THE DEVIL. Oh, the latest fashion among the Life Force fanatics. Did you not meet in Heaven, among the new arrivals, that German Polish madman? what was his name? Nietzsche?

THE STATUE. Never heard of him.

THE DEVIL. Well, he came here first, before he recovered his wits. I had some hopes of him; but he was a confirmed Life Force worshipper. It was he who raked up the Superman, who is as old as Prometheus; and the 20th century will run after this newest of the old crazes when it gets tired of the world, the flesh, and your humble servant.

THE STATUE. Superman is a good cry; and a good cry is half the battle. I should like to see this Nietzsche.

THE DEVIL. Unfortunately he met Wagner here, and had a quarrel with him.

THE STATUE. Quite right, too. Mozart for me!

THE DEVIL. Oh, it was not about music. Wagner once drifted into Life Force worship, and invented a Superman called Siegfried. But he came to his senses afterwards. So when they met here, Nietzsche denounced him as a renegade; and Wagner wrote a pamphlet to prove that Nietzsche was a Jew; and it ended in Nietzsche's going to heaven in a huff. And a good riddance too. And now, my friend, let us hasten to my palace and celebrate your arrival with a grand musical service.

THE STATUE. With pleasure: youre most kind.

THE DEVIL. This way, Commander. We go down the old trap [*he places himself on the grave trap*].

THE STATUE. Good. [*Reflectively*] All the same, the Superman is a fine conception. There is something statuesque about it. [*He places himself on the grave trap beside The Devil. It begins to descend slowly. Red glow from the abyss*]. Ah, this reminds me of old times.

THE DEVIL. And me also.

ANA. Stop! [*The trap stops*].

THE DEVIL. You, Señora, cannot come this way. You will have an apotheosis. But you will be at the palace before us.

ANA. That is not what I stopped you for. Tell me: where can I find the Superman?

THE DEVIL. He is not yet created, Señora.

THE STATUE. And never will be, probably. Let us proceed: the red fire will make me sneeze. [*They descend*].

ANA. Not yet created! Then my work is not yet done. [*Crossing herself devoutly*] I believe in the Life to Come. [*Crying to the universe*] A father! a father for the Superman!

She vanishes into the void; and again there is nothing: all existence seems suspended infinitely. Then, vaguely, there is a live human voice crying somewhere. One sees, with a shock, a mountain peak shewing faintly against a lighter background. The sky has returned from afar; and we suddenly remember where we were. The cry becomes distinct and urgent: it says Automobile, Automobile. *The complete reality comes back with a rush: in a moment it is full morning in the Sierra; and the brigands are scrambling to their feet and making for the road as the goatherd runs down from the hill, warning them of the approach of another motor. Tanner and Mendoza rise amazedly and stare at one another with scattered wits. Straker sits up to yawn for a moment before he gets on his feet, making it a point of honor not to shew any undue interest in the excitement of the bandits. Mendoza gives a quick look to see that his followers are attending to the alarm; then exchanges a private word with Tanner.*